EVERYTHING I WAS, WAS FOR YOU

A STORY OF LOVE REMEMBERED, AND GOODBYES THAT NEVER REALLY ENDED

BRINDA GAHLOT

In the loving memory of my grandfather,

Late Jagdish Kumar Rawat

and my father, Late Satish Gahlot-

You were the first to teach me love, courage, and quiet resilience.

Though you are beyond these pages, every word carries the weight of your memory.

This book is written with a heart that still looks for you in every triumph and every silence.

Contents

Contents

Foreword

I was smiling ear to ear when I received a request from Brinda to write a brief foreword to this book. What more can a teacher ask for than to see his students shine in their own light? She's got wings, words, and that touch of magic.

I am truly at a loss for words. First books are always special you know, much like first love. And first love? It takes us back to those days when emotions feel too big for the heart, when dreams come rushing in without rules, when heartbreaks arrive without warning, and when loneliness tiptoes in at just the wrong time. This book gently pulls us into that wild, beautiful mess. You're right', the bittersweet memories of adolescence; this book brings it all back.

Remember the chaos and the confusion? I know there's no book that can ever fully condense the matters of the heart, but this one comes close. A lot of life happens in these pages.

Everything I Was, Was for You doesn't have a hero or a heroine. It doesn't have villains either. It just has people with questions, promises, and emotions. I wouldn't claim this book has all the answers you're looking for, but just like Riva, the girl in the story, it brings us a little closer to understanding ourselves or what they say these days, rediscovering ourselves.

There's so much more to be felt. I'm sure once you've finished reading, this book will earn the favourite corner of your bookshelf.

Read it with an open heart.
You may come away changed.
~Deepanshu Tanwar

Foreword

Brinda is not just a good friend of mine- she's someone I've seen grow, question, stumble, and rise again, all in pursuit of something most of us quietly run from: self-discovery.

Everything I Was, Was For You is more than just words brought to life. It's the product of countless nights, quiet love, heartbreak, and tears poured onto paper, turning her pain into the pages you now hold. These words carry pieces of her that were never meant to be seen, but had to be written.

It's a piece of her, a vulnerable offering where the lines between truth and fiction blur so seamlessly, it becomes impossible to tell where one ends and the other begins.

She didn't write this book for praise. She wrote it to feel alive, to breathe a little easier, and maybe to remind someone out there that they're not alone.

I feel honored to have witnessed this book being born quietly, painfully and beautifully. It endured more than you'll ever know. And now, it's here ready to be seen.

What you do with it now, that part is yours.
I hope it finds your heart, and maybe even helps you find pieces of your own.
~Astha Talwar

Preface

This book is a journey through fragile hearts, unspoken words, and the chaos that lives within all of us. At its core, it's about love, the kind that is soft and devastating, silent yet screaming, comforting but wild. The characters aren't heroes or villains; they're real, flawed, and human. They fall apart, break promises, and love deeply, but not always rightly.

Told through raw emotions and vivid moments, the story explores what it's like to grow up while carrying wounds you don't yet know how to name. It doesn't promise fairy tale endings but it offers hope, healing, and the quiet strength of facing your own reflection.

It is layered with emotion, and intentionally vulnerable. There's pain here, but also resilience. Through heartbreak and soul-searching, the characters learn what it means to stay, to leave, and to love.

Though fictional, the emotional truths within are universal. This book doesn't just ask to be read, it asks to be felt. It's not about a perfect plot. It's about imperfect people finding meaning in a world that rarely offers easy answers.

It's not just a book. It's a mirror. And sometimes, it reflects exactly what you didn't know you were looking for.

Acknowledgements

There is no story without the hands that hold it together.

To my family, especially my mother, whose endless love has been my foundation, I offer my deepest gratitude. Mom, your quiet strength, your unwavering faith in me, and your gentle presence through every high and low gave this book its spine. Your belief in me, even when I faltered, has been my guiding light.

To my friends, whose encouragement never wavered, thank you for being my constant in a world full of uncertainties and those who read early drafts, you saw what I could not, your insight shaped this story into something I could never have imagined on my own. And to the characters, both real and imagined, whose stories poured into me and demanded to be told: I am forever grateful for your whispers and your silences.

This book is not just mine, it is a collective breath. Thank you to everyone who believed in the words, the dream, and the journey.

Prologue

Some stories don't begin.
They unravel.
     From a silence left too long,
a goodbye that never echoed back,
a memory that kept breathing even after the moment
stopped.
     This one begins somewhere between what was said
and all that never made it out of the heart.
     Not quite a love story.
Not quite a tragedy.
Something messier.
Something real.
     She didn't mean to hold on so tightly.
Didn't mean to fall apart so quietly.
But grief doesn't knock.
And neither does guilt.
     There were messages left unsent.
Hands she let go of too late.
And versions of herself
she never thought she'd have to meet.
     What remained was not a lesson,
but a pulse.
Something soft, unfinished.
Like the closing line of a poem no one heard.
     This is how it all begins-
with everything she was,
for someone she wasn't ready to lose.

"In the end, it was never about being whole. It was about learning how to live with the missing pieces."

CHAPTER ONE

THE RETURN

The train hissed to a stop, exhaling steam like a weary beast. Riva stepped onto the platform, her boots clicking softly against the weathered tiles. A wave of warmth hit her, not just from the summer air that clung to her skin, but from the scent of home, the faint aroma of old metal, roasted peanuts from a nearby vendor, and something vaguely floral that she couldn't name but had missed without knowing it.

Everything looked smaller. The station, the shops, even the trees. As if the town had shrunk in her absence, folding inward like a secret too shy to be told.... Or maybe she had simply outgrown it.

Riva closed her eyes for a moment and inhaled deeply, letting the air of her past settle into her lungs. The wind carried the laughter of schoolchildren from somewhere in the distance. A dog barked. The rhythmic chaos of honking cars reminded her that time had not paused here. Life had continued, steadily, indifferently, while she had been away trying to stitch herself back together in the city.

Her phone buzzed in her pocket. Smiling instinctively, she pulled it out, expecting a warm "Where are you?" from Prisha or maybe a goofy sticker. Instead, a chill ran through her.

Unknown Number: Welcome back, Riva......

She froze.

The smile faltered. Her eyes darted over the platform, scanning for a familiar face or anyone watching too intently. But there was nothing. Just the slow churn of bodies, the clatter of luggage wheels, the shuffle of lives moving forward.

Who would message her like that? And why now, the moment she stepped foot back home....

She shook her head, willing the unease away.

No. She wouldn't let paranoia sink its claws in on her first day back. Not yet.

Tucking the phone back into her bag, Riva walked toward the station's exit, her footsteps echoing louder than they should have. She had more pressing things to worry about—like seeing her parents again, finding her old rhythm, maybe even laughing with Prisha like nothing had changed.

But everything had.......

As she stepped out onto the main street, the world greeted her with a weird sensory punch of nostalgia. The sharp, greasy sizzle of samosas frying at a roadside stall.

A rickshaw sputtering by with too many passengers and too loud a radio. The store where she'd bought her first diary still had the same faded blue sign. An old man on the corner was selling mangoes, just like he had when she was thirteen.

And yet... something felt off.

Like coming home to a familiar melody that was playing in the wrong key.

Riva hesitated for a heartbeat, her hand resting on the handle of her waiting taxi. She glanced over her shoulder, half-expecting someone to be standing there, watching her. But the crowd had already swallowed her up, oblivious...

She slid into the backseat, the door clicking shut behind her with a finality that made her chest tighten.

She was home.

But something-or someone-was waiting for her.....

CHAPTER TWO

FAMILIAR FACES

The cab wound through streets Riva once knew like the back of her hand, but now they felt like a half-remembered dream. The buildings had the same bones, but they'd changed their clothes- new paint, unfamiliar signs, a different energy. Even the banyan tree at the crossroads, once her childhood compass, had been trimmed down, its unruly roots caged in by cement...

She rested her forehead against the cool window glass, watching the town blur past in sun-drenched streaks. A small part of her had hoped time here would stand still, that she could simply slot back into her old life like a missing puzzle piece. But everything had moved on. And so had she...

Her parent's house appeared at the end of the lane, weathered but still standing proud in that quiet, old-world way. The gate creaked open like it remembered her. The porch light left on during the day by habit, cast a soft yellow halo over the faded blue door. Her heart clenched.

The front door flew open before she could knock. Her mother enveloped her in a hug before a word was said, arms warm and trembling....

"You're finally home," her mother whispered, her voice catching in her throat.

"I missed you," Riva mumbled, burying her face into her mother's shoulder, the familiar scent of sandalwood and soap anchoring her like a tether to another life.

Her father lingered by the staircase, smiling with a softness he reserved for quiet moments.

"You've grown thinner," he said, his voice low, betraying concern beneath the casual observation.

"You always say that," she replied, forcing a small laugh. "Maybe you just keep imagining me fatter every year."

They all chuckled, the sound a little too fragile. Riva scanned the living room- same rug, same family photos on the wall, the sofa she'd once sprawled across with her textbooks and heartbreaks. And yet the air felt thicker now, as if holding its breath....

Later that evening, Riva found herself in her old room, which had been kept almost intact, a shrine to a younger self. The bookshelf still held her battered novels and old trophies. A poster of a boyband she no longer listened to curled at the edges, hanging on out of stubborn nostalgia.

She was tracing her fingers along the spines of her books when her phone buzzed again.

Unknown Number: Still love your room? Or are the ghosts too loud now?

Her breath hitched.......

She stared at the screen, willing it to dissolve into nothing. It didn't. The message sat there, too deliberate to be a prank. Her eyes flicked to the window, suddenly alert to every creak and whisper of wind outside.

No name. No reply option. Just a message that felt like fingers brushing the back of her neck

She shut her phone off.

ENOUGH.....

Later that night, when the house had settled into silence, she stood on the terrace, watching the stars—familiar constellations blinking down at her like old friends. But even they seemed more distant than before.

Footsteps clattered on the stairs. She turned sharply.

"Riva?" came a voice, tentative but familiar.

She blinked. "Prisha?"

And there she was- wide smile, messy hair, and a laugh that spilled out before words could. Riva ran to her, and they crashed into a hug that felt like a bridge back to something real.

"You idiot, you didn't tell me you were coming today!" Prisha said, pulling back to inspect her. "God, you look like you've been to war."

"I kind of have," Riva murmured.

They sat down, legs crossed, shoulders touching.

"I missed this," Prisha said.

"Missed you. Even though your cryptic texts were very poetic."

Riva smiled faintly. "Everything feels different. Off. Like I came back to a version of life where someone rearranged all the furniture."

"Well, maybe it's time to shake the dust off and find your new rhythm," Prisha said, bumping her shoulder. "And maybe start with chai and gossip tomorrow?"

Riva hesitated. "Sure. Yeah."

But she couldn't stop the image from forming in her mind—her room, her phone, the message.

Someone knew she was back.

And someone, somewhere, was watching....

CHAPTER THREE

ECHOES OF THE PAST

Riva barely slept. The house was quiet, but her mind wasn't. That message had burrowed itself beneath her skin, repeating in her head like a skipped record.

Still love your room? Or are the ghosts too loud now?

The phrasing haunted her. Not just what it said, but how it knew.

When she finally drifted off, dawn had already begun to stain the sky. She awoke to the scent of brewing tea and her mother humming softly downstairs. The sounds of home. But even that warmth couldn't settle the unease knotting her stomach.

She rolled over, her phone still on the bedside table, powered off. For a moment, she simply stared at it. Then, with a resigned breath, she switched it on.

No new messages. No missed calls. The previous one was gone. Erased completely, as if it had never existed. But she knew what she'd seen.

Downstairs, her mother was setting the table with two cups of chai and a plate of marie biscuits like clockwork.

"You still take it without sugar?" she asked, not looking up.

"Yeah," Riva said, sitting down and wrapping her hands around the warm cup, grateful for the anchor.

"I'm glad you're home," her mother continued, voice soft. "This house feels right again."

Riva wanted to smile, to agree. But her thoughts tugged elsewhere. Later that afternoon, she met Prisha at their old haunt- the faded café near the college, still manned by the same grumpy uncle who never got their orders right but always remembered their names. They took their usual corner table by the window.

"So, tell me everything," Prisha demanded, sipping her iced coffee with practiced drama. "All of it. The city, the job, the heartbreaks- plural, I assume?" Riva laughed, genuine, for a second. "Too much to unpack. The city was fast, the job was consuming, and heartbreak... well, that was just part of the package deal."

"And now you're back. For how long?" Riva hesitated. "I don't know. Maybe longer than I thought."

Prisha raised an eyebrow. "That bad?"

Riva didn't answer. Instead, she looked out the window, eyes tracing the cracks on the pavement, the flutter of a worn-out poster, the familiar chaos of this quiet town.

We "I got a message last night," she finally said, her voice low. "From an unknown number. It said something strange. About my room."

Prisha leaned in. "What did it say?"

Riva recited the words, slow and deliberate.

Prisha's expression darkened. "You're sure it wasn't some weird prank? Maybe someone saw your status—knows you're back?"

"It wasn't public. And the message disappeared this morning. It's like it deleted itself."

A pause. The air between them shifted....

"Do you think it's... him?" Prisha asked, carefully avoiding a name. Riva didn't answer right away. Her fingers tightened around her cup. "I don't know. But it felt... personal." Prisha sighed, leaning back. "We buried all that years ago, Riva. Maybe it's time you actually let it stay buried."

"I thought I had," Riva murmured. "But ghosts don't rot in peace, do they?"

They left the café in a heavier silence. As they parted ways, Riva felt the pull of the past like an undertow beneath her feet. The kind that waits until you're walking alone before it drags you under. Back at home, she paced her room before finally giving in. She opened her laptop and pulled up an old file she hadn't touched in years—something she had buried under layers of distraction: her journal.

She began typing.

Day One:

I returned home.

The air smells the same. The silence is louder. And someone remembers me in a way that makes my skin crawl.

I thought I'd moved on.

But what if the past never let me?

As the cursor blinked on the screen, a faint ping echoed from her phone.

Her heart clenched.
Another message.
Unknown Number:
You always did write when you were scared.
She dropped the phone.....

OLD WOUNDS

The next morning came with an eerie quiet. The kind that didn't feel peaceful- just too still, too measured, like the air itself was holding its breath.

Riva stood in front of the mirror, her eyes scanning the reflection like it might show her something more than her own face. There were faint shadows under her eyes now. Her lips were pressed tight, her shoulders stiff. She looked... haunted.
And somehow, older.
Not in years. In weight.

Her phone lay untouched on the bedside table. That last message echoed in her mind like a heartbeat that refused to slow down:
"You always did write when you were scared."
The implication was unmistakable- whoever it was, they knew her. Intimately. Intricately. The kind of knowing that only came from being close.
Too close.....

She pulled open a drawer, shuffling through old notebooks and forgotten pens until she found it a faded red diary with peeling edges. Her high school journal. Most of it was filled with clumsy poetry and secrets she'd never said aloud. But toward the back, the entries grew darker. Denser. Written in cramped, rushed handwriting that barely looked like her own.

She flipped to the final pages.

"He watches me even when I don't look back."

"He says love doesn't need permission."

"Today, he left a rose on my window, but I never told him where I live."

Prisha says I should tell someone. But what if that just makes it worse?

She closed the diary and held it against her chest, eyes brimming. She hadn't read those pages in years.

Downstairs, the doorbell rang.

Her breath caught.

It rang again, two short chimes, a rhythm that felt strangely familiar.

She made her way down, each step slow, cautious. Her mother had left for the temple, and the house was otherwise empty.

Riva opened the door.

A courier stood there with a package. Small. Brown. No label.

"No sender?" she asked, frowning.

The courier shrugged. "Just told to drop it here. Prepaid."

She took it, closed the door, and placed it on the table. Her fingers hovered over the tape. She knew she shouldn't open it.

But she did.....

Inside was a single item: a hand mirror. Delicately framed in vintage bronze, the glass slightly fogged at the edges. It looked antique. Familiar.

She turned it over. A message was etched into the metal backing in tiny, jagged lettering:

"You always looked for yourself in others. Look deeper this time."

A chill swept through her.

She knew this mirror.

It used to sit on her dressing table in high school, until it vanished. She'd assumed her mother had packed it away or that it broke and was quietly discarded. But here it was, returned like an omen.

She held it up and stared into it.

Her reflection wavered slightly, though the air around her was still.

In the background, just behind her shoulder, a figure moved.

Riva spun around.

Nothing.......

The hallway was empty. Just the wall and the painting of her parents from years ago, slightly crooked. Her hands trembled as she set the mirror down. This was no longer just eerie. It was invasive. Intentional. Calculated.

She picked up her phone. No new messages. But the last one still sat open on the screen, mocking her with its familiarity.

"You always did write when you were scared."
And now... look deeper.
She dialed Prisha.
"Can you come over?"
"You okay?"
"No. Not really."
"I'll be there in ten."

By the time Prisha arrived, Riva had placed the mirror back in the box. The air in the house felt too thick, like it had absorbed her panic.

They sat on the edge of the bed, the package between them. Prisha opened it, lifted the mirror, turned it over.
"Did you show this to anyone else?" she asked quietly.
"No. Just you."

Prisha's eyes were narrowed. Focused. "This looks like it was engraved by hand. Like someone was obsessed."
Riva nodded, swallowing hard. "That's what I'm afraid of."

They sat in silence for a while. Outside, the sun was beginning to set, painting the room in long, golden shadows.

Finally, Prisha spoke.
"There's something I never told you," she said.

Riva looked up. "What?"

Prisha hesitated.

Then: "Back then... when everything happened with him, you remember how I said I didn't know much?"

Riva's breath caught. "Yeah..."

"I lied."

CHAPTER FIVE

THE LIE

Riva stared at Prisha, stunned into stillness. The words echoed like a dropped plate in a quiet room- sharp, sudden, irreversible.

I lied..........

"What do you mean?" Riva asked, her voice hoarse.

Prisha looked away, as if the truth might burn too bright if spoken while meeting Riva's eyes. Her fingers fidgeted with the edge of the mirror box, tracing invisible lines.

"I knew more than I said back then. About him. About what he was doing. I just didn't know how to tell you."

The weight of those words settled between them like a fog that thickened the air.

Riva felt the sting of betrayal tighten in her chest.

"You were my best friend," she whispered.

"If you knew something-anything-you should've told me."

"I was scared too," Prisha said quietly. "He..... he was strange, Riva. Not just obsessed with you. There were things he said to me. Messages. He once asked me what perfume you wore, like I was just another stepping stone to get closer to you. And I didn't know what to do."

Riva's mind swirled. This was a piece of the puzzle she hadn't even known was missing. Back then, everything had blurred- school, the fear, her writing, the silence she was too ashamed to break

"I thought you said he never spoke to you," Riva murmured.

"I lied," Prisha repeated, eyes glistening. "Because I didn't want to be involved. Because I thought if I ignored it, it would stop. But it didn't. It just changed shapes."

Riva's hands clenched into fists on her lap. Her voice, when it came, trembled with hurt.
"You let me think I was alone."

"I was alone too," Prisha said, voice cracking. "He sent me letters once—unsigned, but I knew it was him. I burned them. I didn't want to believe he was real."

They sat in silence, both of them suspended in a memory they had buried for too long. Outside, the evening deepened, casting the room into dusky blue and gold. The kind of light that feels like it's running out of time.....
"Did you recognize the message?" Riva finally asked, nodding at the mirror. "The handwriting?"
Prisha hesitated. Then slowly nodded. "It looks... familiar. Like something from a notebook I saw him carry. Black, leather-bound. He used to scribble quotes in it. Your quotes. Your poems."

Riva felt her skin crawl. "He used to read my writing in class. Said it made him feel 'seen.'"

Prisha glanced toward the box. "Do you think he ever left?"

Riva shook her head slowly. "People like that don't leave. They wait."

And suddenly, she felt it. Not fear exactly, but certainty...

Like the mirror wasn't a warning, but a prologue. Like someone had just reopened a book they never finished, and she was the last chapter.

Prisha leaned forward. "You need to talk to someone. Not just me. The police-"

"And say what?" Riva interrupted. "That someone from my past sent me a mirror and a message that might not even be illegal? That I think someone might be following me again?"

She hated the sound of her own voice- tight with panic, brittle with disbelief.....

"You need to document everything," Prisha said, resolute now. "Every message. Every object. Every shadow that moves wrong. This isn't just in your head, Riva."

She nodded numbly. "I know. That's what scares me."

A long pause..... Then Prisha added softly, "I'll stay over tonight. We can set up cameras. Lock the windows. Just... try to sleep."

Riva wanted to laugh....

"Sleep? What a ridiculous suggestion." But she only nodded, grateful and fraying.

Later that night, long after Prisha had drifted into a guarded sleep beside her, Riva sat in bed, the dim glow of her phone casting pale light across her face.

She opened her Notes app.....
She didn't know why, maybe to feel control. Maybe because writing was the only thing that had ever made her feel real.
And she wrote:
"He waits at the edges of my silence,
dressed in the shadows of who I used to be.
He doesn't knock. He never did.
He just slips in through the cracks I left unguarded.
And he watches me remember."

She stared at the words, heart thudding.
Then the screen flickered.
Once. Twice.
And then, without her touching a thing, a new line appeared beneath her poem:
I always liked when you wrote about me........

CHAPTER SIX

Halfway To Healing

The waiting room was too clean. Too quiet. The kind of sterile that made Riva feel like a wound rather than a person.

She sat perched on the edge of a pale blue sofa, hands folded tightly in her lap, as if by sheer stillness she could keep from unravelling. Her eyes skimmed the room- white walls, framed affirmations, a faint scent of lavender. All curated calm.
She hated it.....

Her name was called gently. Too gently. As if she might break.

Dr. Kaur was warm, maybe in her fifties, with eyes that seemed to absorb more than they showed. She offered a smile that wasn't overreaching, just enough to say I'm listening. You can exhale here.

"So," the therapist began, after they had exchanged the formalities. "Where would you like to start?"

Riva hesitated. Where did it begin? The mirror? The boy in school? Or the way the silence inside her kept growing teeth.

"I've been having trouble sleeping," she said. "Nightmares. And then something... something real happened. Or maybe not. I don't know anymore."

Dr. Kaur didn't interrupt. Just nodded gently, encouraging......

"I got a mirror delivered to me," Riva continued. "No sender. Just a message written on it. The handwriting, it reminded me of someone I used to know. Someone I thought I'd forgotten."

"And this person..." Dr. Kaur said carefully, "was someone who hurt you?"

Riva paused. "He never touched me. Not physically. But he was everywhere. Watching me. Following me. He used to send me messages- notes, poems, sometimes just drawings. Things only I would understand. At first, I thought it was some strange kind of attention. But then it felt like being studied. Like I was being collected."

A shiver passed through her.

"And now?" Dr. Kaur prompted.

"Now I feel like I'm back there again. In that girl's skin. The one who kept quiet because she didn't want to sound dramatic. Because everyone said he was harmless. Brilliant, even. Just a little... intense."

Dr. Kaur leaned in slightly, her voice steady. "Riva, what he did- watching you, invading your space, sending you messages, that's not harmless. That's stalking. And it is traumatic."

Riva swallowed, eyes fixed on the floor.....

"I still think about whether I made it all up. Like maybe I was too sensitive. Maybe I invited it by writing poems he liked. By not rejecting his attention loud enough."

Dr. Kaur's voice was firm now. "You are not responsible for someone else's obsession. Ever.... And this kind of second-guessing? It's exactly what trauma does. It rewrites memory. Makes you question the reality of your own experience."

Riva felt something sharp rise in her throat. Not grief. Not fear. Something older—guilt, maybe. Or shame she hadn't earned but carried anyway.

"I keep thinking," she whispered, "what if he never left? What if he was always waiting for me to come back to myself? What if this-" she gestured vaguely toward the present, the room, the moment "was exactly what he was counting on?"

Dr. Kaur let the silence sit for a moment before breaking it softly. "And what do you want, Riva?"

She blinked. No one had asked her that in a long time.

"I want... peace. I want to not look over my shoulder. I want to feel like I own my life again."

"That's a beginning," Dr. Kaur said. "We can work toward that. But we'll need to dig into the past. Not to relive it, but to reclaim it."

Riva gave a faint nod. Her hands were cold. Her pulse was loud in her ears.

As the session ended, Dr. Kaur handed her a small card. On it, a quote was printed:

"YOU DON'T HAVE TO BE FEARLESS TO BE BRAVE!"

Outside, the sky had turned soft with dusk. As Riva stepped onto the street, the city felt quieter than usual, like it was holding its breath.

Her phone buzzed.

A message. No sender.

Just one line:

Did you tell her about me?

Her heart stopped.

The shadows weren't just outside anymore. They were following her in......

CHAPTER SEVEN

Echoes and Silences

Riva stood in front of it again.

The mirror.

It leaned against the far wall of her bedroom like it had always belonged there. The message, long wiped clean, had left a faint smudge she couldn't scrub away—not from the glass, not from her thoughts.

She stared into it now, studying her reflection as though trying to decode herself.

Who was the girl looking back?

There was something foreign about her, something ghosted around the edges. Her eyes had taken on a new kind of hollowness. Not empty, exactly, but stretched thin, like the light behind them had been tampered with.

She pressed her fingers to the frame. The mirror was cold. Too cold. It didn't belong in this space, in this life she was trying to rebuild. And yet it was here. A silent witness. A relic from a version of her past she never gave permission to return.

Her phone buzzed again.

This time, she didn't want to look. But her body moved before her mind could stop it....

She flipped the phone over.

Unknown Number.

"Do you still write about me?"

Riva's breath hitched. Her thumb hovered over the screen, aching to block, delete, erase—but she didn't. She just stared. The question spun in her head like a slow, cruel wheel.

Do you still write about me?

He knew her weakness. The place she bled most honestly: the page.

The poems, the journals, the unfinished letters. Her memories had always found language before they found peace. And he had read them once, back in school, when she'd foolishly let him.

She didn't write about him anymore. But she wondered now, was he still reading?

She sat at the edge of her bed, phone limp in her hand, and let the thought rot a little in her mind.

He wants to be a character. Not a consequence.

She exhaled a quiet, broken sound.

She picked up her notebook, the one with pages she hadn't dared to fill in weeks. Her pen hovered. Her hand trembled. But she wrote:

"You do not get to live here.
Not in this room,

not in this mirror,
not in the ink of my recovery.
You are a haunting,
not a history."

She stopped. The words stared up at her like brave, defiant things.

And then she turned to the mirror again.

Her reflection looked back, more solid this time. More hers.

Until,

A shadow flickered behind her in the glass.

She spun around.

Nothing.

Just the hum of the evening and the stillness of her flat. Her chest tightened. She glanced at the mirror again.

Empty.... Still.....

Was it the light? Her imagination? Or something more deliberate?

The doorbell rang.

A sharp, short buzz.

She froze.

It was nearly 9 PM. No one ever came by unannounced. Her heart thundered.

The buzzer rang again.

She approached the door slowly, her body tight with dread. She didn't open it. Just pressed her eye to the peephole.

The hallway was empty.

No footsteps retreating. No packages left. Just silence.

And then she heard it.
Tap. Tap.
She turned slowly.

The mirror.
The sound had come from the mirror.
Her breath caught.
She stepped closer. Her pulse roared in her ears. On the glass—barely visible in the faint light—something new had appeared.
A smudge. No letters.
Written in condensation that hadn't been there before.
One word.
"Soon."
She backed away.

The air around her seemed to grow colder, the walls pulling inward. She wanted to scream, to smash the mirror to pieces, but something held her still.
Not fear.
Recognition....
Because deep down, she had always known—he wasn't finished..

CHAPTER EIGHT

THE BIRTHDAY

Riva hated birthdays now.

She used to love them, she used to bake her own cake, light candles just to make a wish even if she didn't believe in them, and dance barefoot in her room with the music too loud and the windows wide open. She used to take photos of the sunset every year on her birthday, as if to mark her own growing up with the sky's.

But not anymore.

Now, birthdays were just a reminder: another year gone. Another year survived, yes- but not quite lived.

She woke up to silence. Her phone had a few obligatory texts. A message from her aunt. A generic "HBD Riva" from a college friend she hadn't spoken to since the last exam. Nothing from her parents. That silence still felt loud, even after all this time.

She sat at her small kitchen table with a cup of bitter coffee and no appetite. She had told no one at work it was her birthday. She didn't want the awkward cake, the paper crown, the sing-song cheer from people who didn't know the first thing about her.

She just wanted the day to pass like a shadow, unnoticed.

But life, or whatever was pretending to be it lately, had other plans.

Around noon, a bouquet arrived at her office.

She stared at it like it was a bomb.

The flowers were fresh. Lilies, her favourite. Tied with a dark blue ribbon and no note.

"Secret admirer?" her coworker teased.

Riva forced a polite laugh, but her stomach had gone cold.

She didn't admire secrets anymore.

She carried the bouquet home that evening, fingers clenched too tightly around the stems. At her front door, she hesitated before unlocking it, a strange tension humming behind her ribs. The mirror had been quiet since that night, but the word-Soon-still hung heavy in her mind like a storm cloud.

She set the flowers down on her kitchen counter. Opened a window. Lit a candle.

Make a wish, something in her whispered.

She didn't.

Instead, she walked to her room and sat on the edge of her bed, staring at the notebook she hadn't touched since the mirror incident.

Then her phone lit up again.

Unknown Number.

She stared at it until it went dark again.

Five seconds later: another message.

"Did you like the flowers?"

Her throat closed. Her fingers moved before she could stop them.

Who are you? she typed.

The reply was immediate.

"You know who I am. You always knew."

Her pulse screamed in her ears. The notebook fell from her lap. She stood and walked to the mirror.

It was clear. Just her reflection. Her hair a little disheveled, eyes dark and tired.

But the fear wouldn't leave her.

Her birthday. Her favourite flowers. A message. A memory trying to be reborn.

She grabbed the bouquet and hurled it across the room.

The glass vase shattered. Water and petals and glass shards scattered like grief across the floor.

Riva stood there, chest heaving, eyes hot and wet.

Happy birthday to me.

And then-

A knock at the door.......

CHAPTER NINE

THE KNOCK

The knock echoed again.

Three slow, deliberate taps.

Riva froze, her bare feet rooted to the cold floor, her heart thudding so violently she could hear it in her ears. She hadn't buzzed anyone in. No one knew where she lived—at least, no one who would send lilies and knock without warning.

Glass shards from the broken vase sparkled at her feet. The room felt too quiet, like the stillness before a scream.

She stepped forward cautiously, her hand brushing against the counter to steady herself. Another knock.

Not loud.

Just certain.

She inched toward the door, each step betraying her calm. She peered through the peephole.

Nothing.

Empty hallway. Dim lights. Quiet as a crypt.

She waited.

Then opened the door.

No one.

Only a small envelope on the ground. Black, with her name written in a script she couldn't mistake.

The same handwriting as the journal.

Her hands trembled as she bent to pick it up. The hallway behind her remained quiet, undisturbed, but every hair on her neck stood up like it was screaming run.

She closed the door. Locked it. Bolted it. Then bolted it again.

Riva sat on the couch, envelope in hand. The silence pressed in tighter than before.

She opened it.

Inside was a single photograph.

A girl- her, at around ten- sitting on a bench in a park she barely remembered. Sunlight in her hair. Smiling, but there was something off in the eyes. Like the smile wasn't hers. A man's hand rested on her shoulder, but the face had been scratched out with something sharp. The photo looked weathered. Old.

Riva turned it over.

crawled on the back, in the same familiar handwriting:

"You promised you'd never forget. But you did. I remember everything."

She dropped the photo like it burned.

What the hell was this?

The journal. The mirror. The dreams. The lilies. The texts. Now this.

Was she losing it?

Or was something trying to be found?

She ran her hands through her hair, trying to breathe.
A flicker caught her eye.
The mirror.

The surface rippled- just for a second. Like a pond disturbed by a single drop.

Riva stood, her limbs heavy, and walked toward it. Her reflection stared back, but her eyes- her reflection's eyes- not her own. Not quite.

Then, clear as water, a word bloomed on the mirror's surface:

"Come."

And below it, a date.

Tomorrow.....

THE MIRROR

She didn't sleep.

She couldn't.... Not with the photograph on her kitchen counter, not with the mirror pulsing like it held a breath too long. The word Come was still there when she returned to it hours later, as though someone had etched it into the glass from the other side of the world.

Below it, the date: April 6.
Tomorrow.
No time. No address. Just that.

Riva sat cross-legged on the rug, the city lights outside her window flickering like the stars had moved downtown for the night. She watched them from the floor, her body still but her mind racing through every corner it could turn.

She tried to rationalize it. Maybe it was a prank. A cruel, calculated game. But no—no one could know what they knew. The handwriting, the photo, the journal that appeared out of nowhere. The lilies.

No one else knew about the lilies.

And no one alive would've had that photo. Not unless they'd been there.

She stared at the mirror again. Her own reflection looked tired- hollow-eyed and pale. But still hers.

Until it wasn't.
A flash. Just a second.
A girl.

The same age as Riva. Same face. But the hair was wet and tangled. A white dress stained at the hem. Eyes dark with something ancient and unreadable. She stood in the same room, but behind her, everything was different- drenched in shadows. Walls weeping. A version of Riva's apartment that had drowned in grief.

The girl blinked, and she was gone.

Riva scrambled back from the mirror like it had tried to reach through and grab her. She hit the couch with a grunt, her breath coming in jagged waves.

She stared at the glass. Nothing but her own face now, shaken and scared.

Something was happening. Something she couldn't explain. Something she might have asked for, even if she didn't remember when or why.

But she knew this much:
She had to go.
Wherever there was.

She didn't know what she would find. She didn't know what part of herself had been left behind in the cracks of that old mirror, in the handwriting of a stranger who knew too much.

But if she didn't go tomorrow-
She might never know.
And maybe, she thought, this wasn't the beginning of madness.
Maybe it was the end of forgetting....

CHAPTER ELEVEN

COLLAPSED BETWEEN YESTERDAYS

The morning arrived like a held breath released.

Muted, grey, and soft at the edges. No birdsong. No sirens. Just the quiet hum of something about to happen.

Riva dressed slowly, her fingers trembling as she fastened the buttons of a loose cotton shirt. She chose white- like a blank page. Like peace. Or surrender.

The photograph stayed in her bag. The journal too. She didn't take much else. It felt wrong to bring things from this world into whatever waited on the other side. If there was another side.

She hadn't told anyone. What would she even say? "I'm going to meet a ghost in a mirror"? "Someone who knows me better than I do myself?"

So she left her phone on the kitchen table, face down, its screen dark.

At 10:24 a.m., she stood in front of the mirror.

The word was still there, faint but unmistakable.

Come.......

And suddenly, her apartment felt too small. Too still. Like it had folded in on itself, trying to trap her in the silence.

She reached out and placed her palm against the glass.

It was cold.

But beneath that cold, something pulsed.

Like a heartbeat.

The surface trembled faintly. Just once.

And then the mirror gave.

She gasped, stumbling forward- not falling through, not quite. It was more like being pulled.

One moment, she was standing in her room.

The next, she was somewhere else.

The air changed.

The walls around her were still- but wrong. Tilted, bruised by time. It was her apartment, and yet it wasn't. The colours were faded, the shadows deeper. Like a memory of a place, not the place itself.

And standing across the room- near the window- was her.

The girl from the mirror.

Not a reflection. Not a dream. A living echo.....

Her hair was loose, longer. Her skin paler, almost translucent. And her eyes- those dark, endless eyes- watched Riva with a sorrow so vast it felt ancient...

Riva didn't speak....She couldn't!

Neither did the other girl.

They just stared.

Two versions of a truth.

Two halves of a loss.

And in that silence, something cracked open between them……

A seam of time.

A memory.

A beginning…….

The silence stretched, not awkward but sacred- like the space between lightning and thunder.

Riva took a cautious step forward.

The other girl mirrored nothing. She remained still, her gaze steady, like she'd been waiting centuries for this moment and wouldn't let it slip too quickly.

"I'm here," Riva whispered, though her voice sounded fragile in this space. "You said... to come."

The girl's lips curved, but not into a smile. It was a sadness so soft, it almost looked like understanding.

"I know," the girl said. Her voice was Riva's voice, only softer—less weighted by this world.

"Who are you?"

The girl tilted her head slightly. "I'm what you left behind."

The words dropped like pebbles into a still lake, rippling through something deep.

"I didn't leave anything," Riva said, defensively. But even as she said it, her throat tightened. "I-"

"You buried it," the girl interrupted gently. "You had to..."

Riva felt a tremor rise in her chest. "Buried what?"

The girl stepped closer now. There was no malice in her movements- only grief and memory. She reached out, but didn't touch Riva. Her hand hovered, inches from her cheek.

"The day the laughter stopped," she said. "The day you stopped drawing stars in the corners of your notebooks. The day your world went quiet."

Riva flinched. She hadn't told anyone about that. Not even in her journal. The stars. The silence.

"You remember?" Riva asked.

"I am the memory," the girl said simply. "And I'm tired of being locked away."

Tears pricked Riva's eyes. Her chest ached like it had been hollowed out.

"You think I wanted to forget?" she whispered. "You think it was easy?"

"No," the girl said. "I think it nearly broke you."

They stood in the dim, echoing version of Riva's apartment- one real, one remembered.

Then the girl stepped aside, and behind her, a door appeared.

Not a door that existed in Riva's world. This one was made of light and shadows, flickering softly like a flame. Carved into the frame were words- not in English, not in any language she knew, but somehow Riva understood:

"To face the truth, step through."

Riva turned to the girl. "What's behind it?"
"Everything you were afraid to feel."

Riva's pulse quickened. She could walk away. She could
return to her apartment, pretend this was a dream, go back
to her job, her lists, her half-slept nights.
But she didn't move.
"I'm scared," she said.
"I know," the girl replied. "But that's the first door."

Riva reached for the handle.
And this time, she didn't flinch...She laughed, and the
sound tried to chase away the heaviness in the air, but it
fell flat, like sunlight failing to warm skin in winter. Her
words were light, but her hands fidgeted, her eyes darted
too quickly. I watched the lie in her smile, and wondered if
she could see the one in mine.

I wanted to stop her, to say something honest- anything-
but the truth was clawing inside my throat, too sharp to
speak without bleeding....

So I let her go....
She left like she had somewhere to be, but the silence
she left behind stayed longer than she ever had.

The room felt unfamiliar once she was gone. My coffee
had gone cold. My thoughts colder.
I went home that evening and stared at the ceiling for
what felt like hours. My phone buzzed with meaningless
notifications. The world kept spinning outside my window,
but mine had tilted just slightly enough to feel it in my
bones.

I changed into a worn T-shirt, switched off the light, and slid under the blanket, hoping maybe sleep would understand what I didn't. But even that came in waves. Restless. Jagged.

I didn't know it then, but that night would be the last one where everything still felt almost normal.

Because by the time I'd open my eyes again,

It would be April 7.

And nothing would ever feel the same again.

CHAPTER TWELVE

THE APRIL THAT CHANGED EVERYTHING

The morning light sifted through the curtains like powdered gold, but it didn't warm her.

Riva lay on her bed, eyes wide open, staring at the ceiling. She hadn't slept, not really. Her mind was still caught somewhere between dream and memory, between the echo of the girl's voice and the shimmer of that impossible door.

It felt like something had shifted inside her like a subtle but irreversible tilt. As if the axis of her being had realigned and the world hadn't noticed.

She reached for her phone. No messages. No missed calls. Not even a calendar reminder. The silence of the digital world mirrored her own- unmoving, detached.

But something in her chest stirred. Not peace. Not quite pain either. It was a presence. A weight that hadn't been there before, or maybe it had always been there and she was just now beginning to feel it.

She sat up slowly, legs dangling over the edge of the bed. The floor was cold beneath her feet.

In the kitchen, she made tea almost automatically, boil water, add leaves, wait for colour, pour. The rituals of waking.
But her hands trembled slightly as she lifted the cup.

She found herself walking to the window. The world outside looked the same- auto rickshaws humming past, a woman haggling with the vegetable vendor, children in oversized uniforms trudging to school. Mundane. Familiar.
And yet, the ordinary looked almost sacred now.

Riva sipped her tea. A single line from the night before kept echoing in her head:
"I'm what you left behind."

She didn't know what the door had done to her, or if she'd even truly walked through it. Maybe it had all been a dream shaped by exhaustion. But there was no denying that something had changed.
There was a pressure building in her, and she couldn't tell whether it was grief rising to the surface or the beginning of healing.

She opened her notebook, the one she hadn't touched in weeks.

She stared at the blank page, pen in hand.
She didn't write lists.
Not today.
Instead, she drew a star.
Tiny. Lopsided. A little shaky.
But a star nonetheless....
And maybe that's what hurt the most—
The fact that it didn't hurt enough anymore.

Riva sat still on her bed, legs folded, thoughts scattered like raindrops on a windshield—blurry, weightless, but impossible to look past. She didn't cry. Not because it didn't ache, but because the ache had learned how to stay quietly. Like wallpaper on her chest.

Outside, the world was calm. Inside, she was too—but in that strange, hollow way calmness sometimes feels like surrender.

She changed into her old cotton tee, the one that always felt like home, even when nothing else did. The bed felt colder than usual tonight. She turned to one side, then the other, chasing comfort in the creases of the sheets.

And just before sleep took her, in that soft in-between space where thoughts blur and feelings sharpen, she whispered into the pillow-

"Maybe tomorrow... something will feel different."
And with that, she let the night swallow her whole.

CHAPTER THIRTEEN

Somewhere Between Us

Riva stood in front of the mirror longer than usual that morning.

She didn't quite recognize the girl staring back.

Same features. Same tired eyes. But something softer in the lines now. Like her reflection had exhaled after holding its breath for far too long.

She brushed her hair slowly, thoughtfully. For once, she wasn't in a rush. Let the world wait.

There was still no clear understanding of what had happened on April 6. No logical explanation. No way to confirm whether it was real or some elaborate mirage her grief had conjured.

But she wasn't questioning it anymore.

There are some truths that don't need proof, only feeling.

She wore a kurta she hadn't touched in months. It was pale blue with tiny silver dots. Her mother used to say it brought out her eyes. When Riva had tried to throw it out last year in one of her silent rebellions, her father had rescued it from the donation pile.

She smiled faintly at the memory.
Today, she'd visit the library.
Not because she had to. But because she wanted to.

The moment she stepped out of the house, a gust of warm breeze brushed against her cheeks, carrying with it the scent of something faintly floral and forgotten like spring.

The rickshaw ride felt less noisy, less jarring. She watched people more closely, the woman feeding stray dogs near the temple, the little boy chasing his shadow along the footpath, the old man selling sugarcane juice from his cart, his hands moving with practiced ease.
Everything felt more vivid. More alive.

Inside the library, the usual hush greeted her like an old friend.
She walked past the aisles, her fingers grazing the spines of books without reading the titles. There was no urgency in her steps.
And then, almost instinctively, she stopped.
"Section F."
A shelf she'd never paid attention to before.

She pulled out a thin, faded book. Its cover was cracked at the edges, the title in delicate, slanted lettering.
"Letters to the Ones Who Stayed."
No author's name.
She opened it.

And there it was.
A letter.

Handwritten. Ink smudged in places, as though the writer had been crying as they wrote.
She read it.
And then another.
And another.

Every letter was to someone who had passed. And every one sounded like something she could have written herself.
"I looked for you in every stranger who smiled at me today."
"I cooked your favourite dish last night and cried into the curry."
"The world moved on. I didn't. But maybe today, I took a step."

Riva closed the book, her throat thick with emotion.
She didn't take it to the counter.
She left it where it belonged.

Back on the shelf, waiting for the next person who needed it.

She walked out of the library lighter. As though the book had taken something heavy from her hands and held it for a while.
That night, she didn't write in her notebook.
She lit a candle.
Placed it by the window.
And sat beside it, in silence.
Just being.

For the first time in a long while, the silence didn't feel empty...

CHAPTER FOURTEEN

THE WEIGHT OF GOODBYES

Riva woke before her alarm, the silence of the room so complete it felt sacred. Her eyes opened to the ceiling she'd stared at for weeks now, but something about this morning was different.

Not lighter. Not easier.
Just... honest.

There were no dreams chasing her, no tightness in her chest, just a strange stillness. Like her body had stopped expecting pain the moment it opened its eyes. And that in itself felt foreign.

She didn't sit up right away. She lay there, tracing invisible stars on the ceiling with her gaze—stars she used to draw in the corners of notebooks when the world felt too loud. Now, even silence had a sound. The sound of not needing to cry.

That was the strangest part.

When she finally rose, she didn't reach for her phone. She reached for the notebook. Not to write, not to confess, not even to reread. Just to touch it.

The spine was worn from nights she'd clutched it like a lifeline. Pages bent, smeared with ink and maybe a little bit of her heart. So many pieces of herself had bled into this book, she wasn't sure where she ended and the paper began.

Today, it felt heavier. Or maybe she was lighter.

By late morning, she left the house with no plan. Her feet knew where to go even if her thoughts didn't.

Nani opened the door in a faded peach saree, her silver hair tied up in a loose bun, eyes as warm as the afternoons of Riva's childhood.

"Tu aayi?" she asked, as if she had always been expecting her.

Riva managed a small, crooked smile. "I didn't know I was coming."

Nani stepped aside, and without a word, they settled in the courtyard under the neem tree. The tree still dropped yellow leaves like secrets. The same cracked cement floor. The same quiet.

"I didn't tell anyone," Riva whispered after a while.

"Tell them what?" Nani asked gently, sipping her chaas.

"That I'm still not okay."

Nani's eyes didn't flinch. "No one is, beta. They just get better at walking with broken parts."

They sat in a silence that didn't demand anything. The kind of silence that lets grief sit down beside you and rest its tired bones.

Nani told her a story from long ago. How she once wandered alone in Surat, too proud to ask for directions. How she got lost and ended up at a temple. How she lit a diya for someone she'd never met. "Sometimes, the soul knows where to go, even when we don't."

Riva looked down at her hands. She had forgotten how small they were when they weren't clenched.

After lunch- simple daal, soft rice, a small spoonful of mango pickle, they moved to the terrace. The sun wrapped itself around Ria's shoulders like warmth she didn't have to earn.

And she breathed.
Really breathed.
Like her lungs remembered how to take in the world without bracing for impact.

She leaned against the railing, watched the neighbourhood stir below-nan old woman drying papads on a rooftop, two kids racing each other with broken kites, the hum of a life she had almost forgotten how to be part of.

She didn't know what pulled the words from her mouth, but they came anyway.

"Thank you."

Not to Nani. Not to God. Not to anyone in particular.
Just... to the moment.
For letting her exist without ache, even if only for a little while.

Back home, her room felt quieter- but not empty. Just paused. Waiting.

She sat at her desk, pulled the notebook toward her, and opened to a fresh page.
No tears today. No confessions.
Just a letter. A soft one. A beginning.

Dear Me,
You didn't think you'd survive this, did you?
But you're still here.
And that is nothing short of a miracle.

She didn't try to write more. She didn't need to.
Some days don't need poems. Some days just need permission to exhale.

She closed the notebook, pressed her palm to the cover, and let her breath settle.
Not healed.
Not whole.
But still here.
And sometimes, that was everything.

CHAPTER FIFTEEN

IN BETWEEN THE LINES

The house was quieter than usual, even with the windows open.

Riva moved through it slowly, almost reverently, like she was stepping through echoes—every wall, every shadow, stitched with the presence of Ayaan. His memory lingered in the air, not loud, not sharp, but soft. Lingering. Breathing.

The echoes weren't as loud anymore. But they hadn't left.

In the kitchen, she made tea.

Not for comfort.

Not out of habit.

But because she simply wanted it.

That, in itself, felt new.

As the kettle began to whistle, she caught her reflection in the window. A fleeting glance. Hair unkempt. Eyes tired but no longer hollow. There was something settling in her face now. Not peace, exactly. But presence. Like someone who had been underwater for a long time and had just remembered how to breathe.

Her phone buzzed.
A message from Harsh.
"Coming by in an hour. Need to talk."
No emojis. No explanation. Just him.

She stared at it for a moment, heart not racing but thudding. Quietly. Heavily.
Not with fear.
Just with the weight of what could be said. Of what might be left unsaid.

When he arrived, she met him at the gate. His steps were slower than usual, his shoulders slightly slouched like someone carrying something they hadn't put into words yet.

They sat in the living room. No music. No distractions. Just the pause between them, waiting.
For a long while, neither of them spoke.
Then, finally, Harsh did.
"I shouldn't have walked away that day," he said, his voice rough at the edges. "I just... didn't know what to do. With the grief. With you. With all of it."

Riva didn't rush to respond. She let the silence hold his words. Let them settle.
He leaned forward, elbows resting on his knees, hands clasped. "I've been thinking about him too. Every single day. I just... didn't think I had the right to say it. It felt like your pain was bigger. More real."

Riva looked at him, her voice quiet but steady. "Pain doesn't have sizes, Harsh. It just... arrives. And it stays until we let it be seen."

He nodded slowly, swallowing hard.

"I miss you," he said finally. "Not just what we were. I miss you. Even like this. Sad. Healing. Messy."

Something in her cracked- not loudly, but gently. Like an old wound letting in sunlight   reached out and took his hand.

Not to erase the past.

Not to fix anything.

But just to say: I see you. Still.

They sat like that for a while. No rush. No expectations. Just two people remembering what it meant to care. Not in spite of the hurt, but through it.

Outside, the sky deepened, and the world turned to silhouettes.

They didn't say what this meant. Didn't try to define what came next.

They just stayed.

And sometimes, that was enough...

CHAPTER SIXTEEN

More Than A Memory

The morning was gold-dusted.

The kind of light that filtered through windows like an old song- familiar, tender, maybe even holy.

Riva stood on the terrace, barefoot, the mug warm between her palms. The chill in the air wrapped itself around her like an afterthought, but she didn't mind. It was the kind of morning that didn't demand anything.

Below, the city was slowly stretching awake- rickshaws coughing to life, a milkman arguing gently with a vendor, the soft blare of an old Kishore Kumar tune floating up from somewhere. And above it all, two kites tangled in the sky like lovers who hadn't learned to let go.

Her chest didn't ache as much today.

The grief was still there, it always would be. But today it was quieter. Less like a scream, more like a hum. A part of her. Not all of her.

She sat down on the terrace floor, tucking her legs beneath her. Her eyes drifted closed, her breath slow and steady, like she was trying to sync herself with the silence around her.

And in that stillness, Ayaan arrived- not in pain, not in memory, but in warmth.
She saw him, clear as day:

Sneaking extra mango slices and acting innocent.
Shouting from the bathroom, "Rivaaaa, where's the shampoo?" even though he knew.
That silly way he said her name when he wanted something: "Riiiii."
The mismatched socks. The stupid dance moves. The dimples.

And for the first time in weeks, she let herself smile.
A real one.

It felt... wrong at first. And then, right.

It didn't feel like forgetting. It felt like remembering differently.

Later, she wandered to the bookstore near the college. She hadn't gone in months. The bell above the door jingled softly, and the owner looked up, recognized her, but said nothing. Just smiled the way people do when they see someone returning to themselves.

She walked the aisles slowly. Her fingers grazed the spines like they were old friends. Then she paused.

A worn copy of The Little Prince.

She opened it at random.

"It is the time you have wasted for your rose that makes your rose so important."

Her throat caught. The words hit her somewhere deep like a truth she hadn't known she was waiting to hear.

She bought the book without thinking.

Not because she needed it.

But because it had found her first.

Outside, the wind stirred her hair, and for a second she could have sworn she felt someone watching. Not in fear. Not like before.

Just a flicker. A memory trying to return. Or maybe asking permission to leave.

She didn't look over her shoulder.

She didn't need to.

Back home, she placed the book gently on her shelf right beside the photo of Ayaan. His eyes smiled back at her from the frame, mischief frozen in time.

She lit a candle. Not out of ritual. Not to summon anything.

But to say:

I'm still here.
And I remember you.
But I remember me, too.

The flame flickered. The room breathed.

And somewhere between love and loss, Ria finally understood that
She wasn't healing despite the grief.
She was healing through it.

Not perfectly.
Not loudly.
But honestly.

And maybe that was enough...

CHAPTER SEVENTEEN

SLIPPING THROUGH MY FINGERS

The air carried the weight of summer.

Heavy. Quiet. The kind of heat that didn't come from the sun, but from the way time lingered too long inside closed walls.

Riva sat by the window, legs folded, her dupatta pooled like fabric fog in her lap. The light spilled across the floor like liquid gold, slow and unbothered. Outside, the world moved in its usual rhythm- cars honking, children yelling, vendors calling out prices like nothing had changed.

But inside the house, time moved differently.

Slower.
Tender.
Suspended.

It had been five days since that morning on the terrace. The morning where laughter slipped from her lips without warning. She hadn't laughed since. But she hadn't broken either.

She was floating somewhere in between.

A knock broke the silence.

"Riva?" Her mother's voice, muffled through the half-closed door.
"Hmm?"
"Papa and I are going to the temple. You'll come?"
Riva hesitated.
A few months ago, she would've gone without thinking. Without feeling.
But she wasn't made of auto-responses anymore.
"I think I'll stay in today," she said softly.
Her mother didn't push. Just offered a quiet, "Okay, beta," and left.
When the door clicked shut and silence returned, it didn't feel lonely. It felt honest.

Riva stood, almost on instinct, and walked to her cupboard. She reached for the old wooden box tucked behind faded clothes and forgotten scarves.

She hadn't opened it since... since the world changed.

Inside were Ayaan's things. Not the obvious ones. Not the photos or clothes or condolence cards.

Just the small things. The ones that didn't mean much to anyone else.

A half-used pen.
A keychain he never used.
A movie ticket with a torn corner and faint grease stains-one of those nights they watched a terrible film and ended up sneaking into another just to make the memory better.
And a sticky note, crumpled, smudged with age:
"Buy shampoo. Don't forget. I'll check."

She stared at his handwriting for a long time. The letters were crooked. Rushed.
Alive.
And suddenly she couldn't hold it in.

The sob came quietly, no shaking shoulders, no gasps for air. Just a sound that came from the center of her.

"I miss you," she whispered.
Again, softer: *"I miss you."*

The words hung in the air like incense. Like prayer. Not desperate. Not dramatic. Just... true.

She held the Post-it to her chest and let the silence absorb her.

This was her temple.

This moment.
These things.
This ache.

Later, when the shadows lengthened across the floor, Ria carefully folded the note and placed it in the drawer beside her bed.

She wasn't ready to let go.

But maybe she was learning how to hold on differently.

Just as she turned to switch on the lamp, her eyes caught the edge of the mirror on the wall.

She hadn't looked at it in days.

Not since-

She didn't step closer. She didn't touch it.

But for a moment, the glass seemed... stiller than usual. Not empty. Just watching.

She looked away. Not out of fear. But out of choice.

She had her own reflection to hold now.
And maybe that meant something.

CHAPTER EIGHTEEN

A SKY FULL OF QUESTIONS

The morning arrived quiet and unsure, like it hadn't made up its mind whether to be gentle or cruel.

Light crept through the curtains in soft pastels- blue, peach, gold. The kind of sky that looked like it belonged in a painting, not a world like this.

Riva lay awake, her eyes fixed on the ceiling, unmoving.

She wasn't sad.
She wasn't fine.
She was... waiting.

For what, she couldn't name. But the stillness in her chest told her something was coming.

Outside, the world stirred as it always did- birds shrieking, scooters starting, someone yelling about milk prices. But inside her, everything was hushed. Like her mind had hit pause.

She stepped out onto the balcony and let the breeze tug at her hair. It smelled faintly of wet cement and something floral.

Jasmine?

Or memory?

She reached for her phone, not out of habit, but because she felt it was time.

One message.

Dhanashree.

"Hey. There's something you should know."

Her chest tightened.

They hadn't spoken in weeks, not since the words they flung at each other like knives. Not since silence filled the space that used to be friendship.

She stared at the screen. Her thumb hovered. Then:
"What?"

A pause. Then-
"Not on text. Can we meet?"

Everything inside her recoiled.
And yet... leaned forward.

Her heart pulsed against her ribs- not with fear. With memory.

She typed slowly.

"Okay. Where?"

The café was one they had never been to before. Neutral ground. No shared laughter embedded in the walls. No ghosts in the cushions.

Riva arrived first and chose a corner table- half-shaded, half-lit. It felt like the safest place to be unsure.

When Dhanashree walked in, she looked... older. Not by age. By eyes. She had always been confident, sharp-tongued, composed. But today, her shoulders looked less proud. Her eyeliner was uneven.

"Hey," she said, sitting down.

Riva nodded. "Hi."

They didn't smile. Not out of coldness. Out of respect, for everything that had broken between them.

"I don't know where to start," Dhanashree said, fingers fumbling with her bracelet.

"You wanted to talk," Riva offered gently. "So talk."

Dhanashree inhaled deeply. "I was angry. And unfair. And I took it all out on you."

Riva blinked. She hadn't expected an apology, not this early. Not this honest.

"I didn't know how to lose him," Dhanashree continued. "And you seemed so... composed. Like it didn't wreck you."

"I wasn't composed," Ria said, a small, tired smile curling at the edges. "I just wrecked quieter."

Their eyes met across the table. And in that look, something cracked.

Not apart.

Open.

"I missed you," Dhanashree whispered.

"I missed you too," Riva admitted.

For a while, they just sat. No performance. No rewinding. Just two girls sitting in the ashes of something they had loved, both too tired to pretend they hadn't bled.

When they stepped out of the café, the sky had begun to cloud.

Riva tilted her head to the wind. There it was again- that scent. That shift.
She glanced over her shoulder.
Nothing.
No shadow.
No figure.
Just the weight of something watching.

That night, she returned home to a room that felt a little less sharp.

She lit her bedside lamp, changed into her softest T-shirt, and crawled under the blanket like it might remember how to hold her.
Just as her eyes began to blur with sleep, her phone buzzed.
Once.
A number she didn't recognize.
She froze.
Then reached for it.
No message. Just a blank screen.

But on the mirror across the room- clear, unmistakable- was a single fingerprint.

On the inside.

CHAPTER NINETEEN

PIECES OF YESTERDAY

The day began like most others- quiet, sun-warmed, soft but inside Riva, everything felt too loud. Her dreams had been too sharp, memories cutting through her mind like glass. She sat on the edge of her bed with her knees curled to her chest, the blanket tangled around her ankles like a shadow she couldn't shake off.

The walls of her room, once familiar, felt like they were listening. Not threatening. Not judging. Just waiting. Waiting for her to speak. To scream. To break.
But she didn't.

She reached for the cup of tea Prisha had left on her table. It had gone cold, untouched. Like the past few days. Like her own voice.
Her eyes fell on the mirror.
Again.

It stood still in the corner of the room, innocent in its frame, yet there was something about it- something that refused to let go. She hadn't seen anything unusual lately. No fingerprints. No flickers. No blurred outlines behind her reflection.

But she knew.

It wasn't about the mirror anymore. It was about what it had reflected back at her for weeks- her fear. Her silence. Her unraveling.

She pulled the curtains shut.

Enough of that.

Downstairs, the house was still. Prisha had gone out. Her parents had left early for work. It was just her now, her and the silence, as always.

She made herself breakfast, though the toast turned soggy under her fingers and the butter refused to melt. She ate it anyway. Because today wasn't about taste. It was about proving she still could.

She sat at the dining table for a long time after that. No music. No phone. Just her, the ticking clock, and the weight in her chest.

Then she walked into Ayaan's room.

She hadn't stepped in since his things were packed away. It still smelled like him- earthy, clean, a mix of books and musk and the old cologne he never stopped using. She walked to the bookshelf, ran her fingers over the titles he used to reread, then knelt to the lowest drawer.

And there it was.

His old notebook.

She didn't know why she opened it. Maybe to hear his voice again. Maybe to finally close the door.

She flipped through the pages- mostly blank, except for one near the middle. His handwriting.

"She doesn't know how much she holds. How much I need her to stay. But I can't say it. I don't want to become another thing she feels responsible for."
Her chest tightened.

It had always been there- the guilt. The weight of things unsaid. The conversations they buried under banter. The love they pretended wasn't fragile.

She traced the words with her fingertips, then hugged the notebook to her chest.

And cried.
Not violently. Not loudly.
Just enough to feel real.

CHAPTER TWENTY

BRUSIED BUT BREATHING

She had been having quieter days.

Ones where the grief didn't scream quite so loudly.

Ones where the world didn't press in on her from all sides.

She was learning how to sit with silence without fearing what might rise from it.

But peace, she'd learned, was never permanent.
It came in flashes. Like weather.
And just as quickly, it could vanish.

And then, just like that-
The call came.

A voice she didn't know, saying Joel's name like a question and an apology all at once.

An accident.
A head injury.
The name of a hospital, tangled in static and urgency.

That was all she could remember. The rest blurred.

It felt like being flung underwater- sounds distorted, limbs weightless, panic blooming like a bruise beneath her ribs. Her body moved, but her mind wasn't sure where it was going.

Now, this corridor.

Long. Lifeless. Humming with that too-clean hospital silence. The kind that doesn't soothe. The kind that makes everything feel too still.

The antiseptic clung to her skin like guilt.

She turned the final corner, her breath catching.

Room 302.

The number etched on the cold metal plaque stared back at her like a dare.

Her heart thudded. Not in rhythm. Not steady. Just loud.

Her hand hovered mid-air, trembling like the door might recoil from her touch. Through the narrow glass panel, she saw him.

Joel.

Still. Pale. Wrapped in hospital white that looked too clinical to belong to someone so full of life.

Her knees nearly buckled.

She pushed the door open.

The smell of disinfectant hit her hard, pulling her deeper into the moment she hadn't been ready for.

Joel didn't look like himself.

His stillness was the cruelest part. Like someone had frozen him in time.

She stepped toward him, her fingers reaching, then hesitating. Then resting gently over his.

Cold.

Not lifeless.

But far from the warmth she knew.

"I'm here," she whispered, her voice tight. "And I'm not going anywhere."

The machines responded in soft beeps and blinking lights. But Joel didn't.

She pulled the chair closer, sitting at his side, folding into herself like something fragile.

Her forehead brushed against the back of his hand. And then- floodwater.

Memories.

His crooked smile.

The way he'd ruffle her hair just to annoy her.

The stupid puns. The late-night calls. The way he made everything seem lighter than it was.

And all the things she never said.

The weight of them curled in her chest like fire.

"You idiot," she breathed. "Always late. Always texting back hours later. But this? This is too far."

A broken laugh escaped her lips. It hurt more than it helped.

"You don't get to do this," she whispered. "You don't get to make me care like this and then just—vanish."

Stillness.

The kind that fills a room and drains you with it.
The door creaked, and her father peeked in. His face was lined with worry, but softened by relief.

"He's stable now," he said quietly, stepping inside. "Doctors say it was a head injury. No internal bleeding. He might wake up in a day or two."

Riva didn't look away from Joel.
She nodded.
Tears slipped down her cheeks, quiet and unannounced.
"I'll wait."
She didn't ask how long.
Some waits aren't timed. Some just exist.

Her father rested a warm, grounding hand on her shoulder before leaving her alone again. Alone with this boy she didn't know how to define, but somehow couldn't imagine not holding onto.

She stayed.

As the sky outside shifted from burnt orange to indigo, and the city exhaled into the night- sirens in the distance, headlights sliding across sterile tiles, she didn't move.

Her fingers stayed laced with his.
Not to anchor him.
To anchor herself.

Because *sometimes, love wasn't a declaration. It wasn't grand or dramatic or wrapped in flowers and promises.*

Sometimes, love was this-
    One breath.
One touch.
One silent vow to stay.

CHAPTER TWENTY-ONE

WHEN THE WORLD PAUSES

Hospitals didn't breathe the way homes did.
They stood still. They watched. They waited.

The silence wasn't gentle here. It wasn't soothing. It was too clean. Too practiced. The kind of quiet that stretched and held its breath.

Riva sat beside Joel's bed, her back curved in the shape of exhaustion. Every inch of her ache- from her neck to her knees to the parts of her heart she didn't know had names. But she didn't complain. She didn't even speak. Her presence had become her language.

She had been whispering to him for hours earlier- tiny pieces of herself, of the world outside these walls.
About the rain that morning. The way it had smelled like earth and memory.
About Dhanashree's message at midnight:
"I hope he's okay. And I hope you are too."
That one had broken her in the softest way.

Because to be seen like that, in the middle of such raw, helpless waiting, it was like someone had cupped her bruised heart in their hands without asking anything of it.

Now, she sat in the quiet.

Her words had frayed at the edges, worn down by time and the unanswered silence that kept stretching between her and the boy lying motionless beneath the white sheets.

Joel.

He looked like a stranger now. So still. Too still. The boy who couldn't sit still in class for five minutes. The boy who used to hum off-tune songs just to irritate her.

Now- this. A body in a bed. A story mid-sentence.

"I don't know how to do this," she whispered, her hand resting on his. "I don't know how to sit beside someone and not know if they're coming back."

She swallowed hard.

"I thought I'd be okay. I thought I could handle this. After Ayaan... after everything... but I'm not okay, Joel. I'm not anything."

The beeping monitor stayed steady. Unbothered. Indifferent.

She hated it.

She hated how it spoke in numbers when she was spilling out everything she didn't know how to hold.

The night curled around her slowly. The hospital lights dimmed. Time lost shape.

And just when she thought she might dissolve into sleep or panic or both—
Something shifted.
A twitch.
Tiny. Barely there.
But real.
She blinked. Sat upright.
Then- again. His fingers. A flicker of life.

Her breath stopped. Her hands trembled.
"Joel?"
No response. But his eyelids fluttered- like curtains in a half-opened window.
Her voice cracked. "Joel, it's me. I'm here."

His lips moved, just slightly. No sound. But they moved.

She leaned closer. "You're okay. You're safe. I'm here."
Then, he opened his eyes.
Slowly. Glazed. Confused.
But he opened them.
He looked at her. Not through her. Not past her.
At her.

"You came," he whispered, barely audible.

Riva's face crumpled as a sob broke from her chest- half joy, half exhaustion.
"Of course I came," she choked out. "Where else would I be?"
His eyes drifted. A ghost of a smile touched his mouth.
"Don't cry," he breathed.
She laughed, a wet, broken sound.

"Too late," she said, pressing her forehead to the back of his hand, her shoulders shaking.

"You're such a mess," he mumbled, his voice fading.

She didn't let go. "So are you."

But he was warm again.

And the silence that had held her hostage for days finally exhaled.

CHAPTER TWENTY-TWO

WHAT WE HOLD ON TO

The day passed in slow waves.

Joel drifted in and out of sleep. The hospital moved around them- nurses came in quietly, doctors murmured in the hallway, trays clinked. The outside world tried to keep its rhythm, but inside this room, time bent.

Riva stayed.

She barely moved from her chair, even though her spine ached and her eyes burned. But the knot in her chest had loosened- just a little. Enough to breathe without feeling like each inhale was a battle.

He was still here.
That was enough.

He stirred in the afternoon, blinking slowly, his voice rasping like rusted hinges. "You didn't go home?"

Riva smiled faintly, brushing a loose strand behind her ear. "Didn't feel right."

Joel squinted at her, trying to read her face. "You look exhausted."

She snorted, the sound light but worn. "You're literally the one in the hospital bed."

He gave a crooked smile. "Touché."

There was a pause.

The comfortable kind. The kind that sits between two people who've been through too much to fill every silence with words.

He exhaled. "It's all blurry. What happened?"

"You fell," she said softly. "Hit your head."

"Right." His eyes drifted. "Guess I always had a thick skull."

She chuckled gently. Then said nothing.

Some silences didn't need fixing.

Later, when his mother arrived, Riva stepped outside. The corridor was bright and cold. The kind of cold that felt like it lived under your skin.

She stared out the window for a while, watching the way the clouds moved without urgency.

Then she texted Dhanushree.

He's awake.

The reply came within seconds.

Thank God. Want company?

She typed. Deleted. Typed again.

Not yet. Soon.

There were still things settling inside her. Still pieces that hadn't landed yet.

That evening, she sat beside him again.

The room had quieted. The harsh light above had been turned off, leaving only a soft lamp near the sink. Joel looked better. His skin wasn't as pale. His voice had gained weight again.

"You stayed," he said quietly.
She nodded.
"Why?"
The question was gentle. Not accusing. Just open.
She swallowed. "Because I couldn't not."

Joel's eyes searched hers, something raw flickering behind them.

"I don't know what we are," she continued. "I don't know if we're anything anymore. But I care about you, Joel. I never stopped."

Her voice broke near the end. But she held it together.
Joel looked at the ceiling.
"I thought I pushed you too far away."
"You did," she said honestly.
He winced. But he didn't look away.

She leaned forward, softer now. "But not far enough to make me stop showing up."
A beat of silence passed.
Then- he reached for her hand.
This time, his fingers were warm. Steady.
She let him hold it.
The nurse came in to adjust his IV. Riva stepped aside.

Before she could leave, Joel spoke again. "Will you come tomorrow?"

Riva looked back at him. And smiled.

Not a bright smile. A quiet one. Tired. Earnest.

"I'll come for as long as you need me."

Later, as she stepped into the night air, the sky was smeared in indigo and lavender.

The city didn't stop. The lights still flickered. But something inside her felt lighter.

For the first time in a long while, she wasn't carrying everything alone.

CHAPTER TWENTY-THREE

THE PLACES WE RETURN TO

The hospital smelled less sterile the second time around.

Or maybe Riva had just stopped noticing.

Maybe her senses had numbed to the white walls, the beeping machines, the way the air always felt filtered and slightly too cold. Maybe, after days of waiting and wondering, this place had softened at the edges- not in comfort, but in familiarity.

She stepped into Joel's room carrying a small box- the kind he once hoarded in the back of her kitchen cupboard when no one was looking. His favourite cookies.

He chuckled, weak but genuine, when she placed it in his lap. "You remembered."

"I forget a lot of things," she said, pulling the chair close. "But not this."

Joel looked better now.

Still pale, still tired, still bruised by whatever hit his skull and whatever cracked between them in the months before, but better. His hair was a messy nest. His voice still rasped, but it had warmth. The sarcastic glint in his eyes was returning, flickering like an old lamp trying to glow again.

They sat in easy silence for a while. Riva watched the light shift on the wall. Joel fiddled with the box, opening it slowly like it might vanish if he moved too fast.

Eventually, they talked.
Nothing heavy. Nothing painful.

They talked about memes. That one senior who snored through a presentation. A teacher who always said "literally" too much. It was light. Strange, even. But it felt sacred like laughing in a place built to hold pain.

Then Joel said, almost out of nowhere, "Dhanushree texted me."
Riva blinked. "Really?"
He nodded. "Asked if you were okay."
She hesitated. "You two talk?"
"Sometimes. Not like before. But... we're trying."

She nodded slowly. "It's weird, isn't it? How grief rips people apart. But it's the silence after that really finishes the job."
Joel didn't respond right away. Just stared at his hands. Then said,
"Do you think we can ever go back?"
She thought about it.
The friendships. The versions of themselves before the loss. The way they laughed without a second thought.

"No," she said. "But maybe we don't have to."

Joel looked at her.

"Maybe we build something else," she continued. "Out of the wreckage. Out of what we still have."

He smiled. A real one this time.

"You sound wiser."

"I broke," she said. "That tends to happen."

On her way home, Riva didn't take an auto. She walked.

The streets looked the same- the tea stall, the half-torn posters on the wall, the stone bench under the banyan tree where Ayaan once threw a samosa at Joel for finishing his chutney.

She didn't avoid the memories. She didn't hold onto them either.

She just walked through them. Like rooms in a house she once lived in.

At night, she lay on her bed, listening to the ceiling fan hum its song.

The weight in her chest hadn't vanished.

But it wasn't suffocating anymore.

And sometimes, that was enough.

CHAPTER TWENTY-FOUR

EVERYTHING I WAS, WAS FOR YOU

The café was still there- nestled between a dusty old bookstore and a flower shop that always smelled like first rain and endings.

Riva hadn't been here in months.

The bell above the door jingled as she stepped inside, soft and familiar. Like an old song humming in the bones.

Dhanushree was already at their usual table, two steaming cups placed neatly in front of her. Masala chai. No sugar in one.

Riva slipped into the seat across from her. "You remembered."

"I didn't know if you'd come," Dhanushree replied.

"I didn't know if I could," Riva said honestly.

They sat there, letting the chai warm their palms but not their words.

"I hated you," Dhanushree said after a moment. "For a while."

"I hated myself more," Riva said, without flinching.

Their eyes met—not sharp. Not soft. Just real.

"I thought ignoring it would make it hurt less," Dhanushree said. "Like if we pretended long enough, the memories would quiet down."

"Did it work?" Riva asked.

Dhanushree smiled sadly. "Not even close."

Riva nodded. "Me neither."

Silence.

Then Dhanushree reached across the table, her fingertips brushing Riva's.

"I don't want to pretend anymore," she whispered. "He existed. He mattered. He changed us."

Riva's throat tightened. "He was everywhere. And then suddenly... nowhere."

"I hear him in my voice sometimes," Dhanushree said. "The sarcastic one. You know the one."

They both laughed. And cried. At the same time.

Later, they wandered into the bookstore next door. It still smelled like ink and dust and old summers.

Riva found a copy of the book Ayaan once teased her for loving.

She held it in her hands. Read the blurb. Then put it back.

Some memories don't need to be owned. Just acknowledged.

"I'm thinking of starting therapy," Dhanushree said suddenly, running her fingers over a row of titles.

Riva turned. "Really?"

"I'm tired," she admitted. "Of carrying it all. I want to lay it down somewhere."

"That's brave."

"You should try it too."

Riva didn't respond right away. But something about the idea lingered. Softly. Not like pressure. Like permission.

When Joel was discharged a week later, Riva was there helping him down the hospital steps, one hand steady on his back.

"Are we... okay?" he asked.

She looked at him.

"We're something," she replied. "And maybe that's enough for now."

He smiled. That crooked, annoying, wonderful smile she didn't realize she'd missed.

"I missed you," he said.

"I missed me too," she whispered.

And maybe that was the truest thing she'd said all year.

That evening, as the sun spilled gold across her windowsill, Riva opened her journal.

The old page was still there:

I miss him.

But I'm tired of being the only one who says it.

She didn't cross it out.

She didn't rip it up.

She turned to a new page.

And wrote:
We still miss you.
But now we say it out loud.
We laugh. We cry. We remember.
And somehow... we live.

The End....

"Everything I Was, Was for You..."

A Letter That Was Never Sent

Dear Ayaan,

If I could gather every word we never said, every silence that stretched like a road between us, I'd tie them into a garland and hang them above our door. Let the wind read them aloud- softly, like prayer.

We didn't meet by chance. We met because something in me knew how to find something in you. Maybe it was the brokenness. Maybe it was the beauty after.

You were never the storm.

You were the hand that held me through it.

And now, the rain doesn't frighten me.

Now, when thunder cracks, I smile.

Because I know what it led me to.

To us.

Love is not always fireworks.

Sometimes it's a warm cup of chai after a long day.

Sometimes, it's forgiveness, quiet and trembling.

Sometimes, it's just showing up again and again until it becomes home.

This is that kind of love.

The kind that stays.

Always,

Riva

"The endings we fear the most are often the beginnings we've been waiting for"

About The Author

Brinda is a young writer from Delhi, currently studying in 11th standard. Writing, for her, was never just about words- it was survival, an alchemy of pain and hope woven into stories. A volunteer with the Art of Living for the past three years, she learned how calm can be carved out of chaos and how sometimes the quietest battles are the ones that change you the most.

Everything I Was, Was for You is her debut novel- a fictional world born from very real emotions. She wrote this story like walking barefoot through fire: losing herself in it, bleeding for it, and somehow, healing because of it. Brinda isn't here to claim greatness. She's here simply because she believed that maybe, through the broken pieces of her words, someone else might find their reflection.

This is her first offering to the world- raw, imperfect, and real, just like all the best things are....